MISSION
CATASTROPHE

Sussex

Edited By Megan Roberts

First published in Great Britain in 2019 by:

Young Writers
Remus House
Coltsfoot Drive
Peterborough
PE2 9BF
Telephone: 01733 890066
Website: www.youngwriters.co.uk

FOREWORD

Young Writers was created in 1991 with the express purpose of promoting and encouraging creative writing. Each competition we create is tailored to the relevant age group, hopefully giving each student the inspiration and incentive to create their own piece of work, whether it's a poem or a short story. We truly believe that seeing their work in print gives students a sense of achievement and pride in their work and themselves.

Our Survival Sagas series, starting with Mission Catastrophe and followed by Mission Contamination and Mission Chaos, aimed to challenge both the young writers' creativity and their survival skills! One of the biggest challenges, aside from facing floods, avoiding avalanches and enduring epic earthquakes, was to create a story with a beginning, middle and end in just 100 words!

Inspired by the theme of catastrophe, their mission was to craft tales of destruction and redemption, new beginnings and struggles of survival against the odds. As you will discover, these students rose to the challenge magnificently and we can declare *Mission Catastrophe* a success.

The mini sagas in this collection are sure to set your pulses racing and leave you wondering with each turn of the page: are these writers born survivors?

CONTENTS

Willow Shoubridge (13)	65
Chloe Gray (13)	66
Lucien Bourgeois-Templeman (11)	67
Edi Xavier-Venn (12)	68
Will White (12)	69
Seb Sommerville (12)	70
Willem Gregson (13)	71
Cameron Laing (13)	72
Rory Macleod (12)	73
Sam Chamberlain (13)	74
Jacob Sayers (12)	75
Alastair Orwin (13)	76
Poppy Mae Kinch (12)	77
Timon Gajos-Weston (11)	78
Kieran Payne (12)	79
Amelia Feldwicke (11)	80
Lucy Scrase (12)	81
Jim Goodyer (12)	82
Felix Holt (11)	83
Aidan Bradley (12)	84
Evie Head (12)	85
Harry Michael Junior Newton (12)	86
Brogan Peters (11)	87
Oscar Hart (11)	88
Tom Laurence Laver (12)	89
Adam Langridge (11)	90
Harry Boreham (11)	91
Beau Kidd (12)	92
Mia Johns (11)	93
Iona Hainge (12)	94
Harry Barnard (11)	95
Molly Brown (11)	96
Jasmine Blake (11)	97
Alex Heasman (13)	98
Jacob Arbuthnot (11)	99
Noah Mason (11)	100

Owlswick School, Lewes

Harvey Buckwell (13)	101
Jack Mead-Pearce (13)	102
Jamar McGlashan (14)	103

St Richard's Catholic College, Bexhill-On-Sea

Izehi Ebhohimen (14)	104
Joshua Porter (12)	105

St Wilfrid's RC School, Southgate

Zachary George Charman (13)	106
Tanya Sunny (13)	107
Lucy Allen (13)	108
William Atkinson (12)	109
Aaron Wright (12)	110
Mason Slight (13)	111
Adam Houas (12)	112

Steyning Grammar School, Storrington

Patsy Burley (11)	113

The Eastbourne Academy, Eastbourne

Tristian Berwick (13)	114

The Gatwick School, Crawley

Isabelle Clark (11)	115
Leilani Campbell-Salmon (12)	116
Madison Membry (12)	117
Katie Steere (14)	118
Zuleika Janay Skuse (15)	119
Evie Jackson (12)	120
Zanab Fatima (11)	121
Aqsa Akbar (12)	122
Evan Mills (11)	123
David Patrick (13)	124
Leo Alexandre Scarborough Gomes (12)	125
Ethan William Wallace (12)	126
Stephanie Gonçalves Da silva (14)	127
Maddison Perry (12)	128
Lucy Elliott (11)	129

THE MINI SAGAS

The Book

Shambling from one side of the room to the other, Oliver Wick pushed his gold-rimmed glasses up the bridge of his nose, a book in his hands reading, 'The doom is near, the meteor shower starts' and yet, he kept reading it over and over again.
"It can't be, not now..."
Boom!
Oliver jumped and ran towards the window, witnessing the chaotic flames outside his door. Fiery meteor after meteor crashed to the ground like a pegasus with injured wings. He turned the final page, flames starting to swallow him whole in seconds. He gasped, reading, 'too late'.

Molly-Rose Coulter (14)
Brighton Aldridge Community Academy, Brighton

Doomsday

It all starts on doomsday, the day Earth almost was erased. A blistering, scorching meteor lunges towards the lava-spilling, bubbling volcano. It looms as the flash streams down from the thunder in the sky. In the blink of an eye, the blazing meteor smashes into the unpredicting, parched volcano. *Boom!* The searing volcano erupts with treacherous sparks streaming upwards into the thunderous sky, causing a monstrous flashing light. The volcano blasts, demolishing anything in its process. As the volcano blazes up, it makes ashy smoke, making the air unbreathable, eliminating any living thing in its way...

Grace Muller (12)
Brighton Aldridge Community Academy, Brighton

Tornado

One day, a small girl called Ashly lived on a farm. On the farm, they had a minotaur, he was big. A tornado came one day, it was bad. The minotaur got sucked up!

"Oh no!" said Ashly.

"Ash! Please!" said Corban.

The minotaur was in front of her.

"Don't go..."

She was sucked up! The minotaur reached and nearly grabbed Ashly's hand, but missed. She screamed, her bow left her head. Ashly was fading in and out of consciousness. The minotaur reached again, this time, he grabbed her. Ashly then fell asleep forever...

Kaieesha Dunn (12)
Brighton Aldridge Community Academy, Brighton

Daredevils

As it hit the floor in front of the school, reds, oranges and yellows exploded around them. The teens had terror-filled eyes. Everyone backed away, fear filling them all, except two: Xyler and Jacy stayed watching the scene, not in terror but in determination. The daredevils wanted to know what it was like outside. Sprinting down the school hallways, Xyler and Jacy ran outside, shoving the main entrance doors open. They both stepped into the misty atmosphere. The floor had been turned into rubble. Ash covered the once-green grass. Suddenly, everything went black...

Paige-Leigh Pettit (14)

Brighton Aldridge Community Academy, Brighton

4

The Ending

It was dark out, there was nobody about. She suddenly heard a noise, a noise she had never heard before. It was a cracking sound. As she went to step outside, she saw something glowing, but it wasn't too far away. She didn't know what it was at first, but then she realised that it was an earthquake. It grew bigger and bigger. She ran back inside and screamed, "Earthquake!" but nobody seemed to believe her.

She ran back out and all she saw were people falling down. She looked to see that the earthquake was approaching...

Erin Jennings (14)
Brighton Aldridge Community Academy, Brighton

Horrendous Hurricane

Crash! Trees swooped throughout the air as fellow citizens screamed in panic. I could hear myself telling myself it would be alright, but I was going crazy, so I wasn't sure. All of a sudden, I heard large, pounding footsteps shake the ground, almost like an earthquake. A hurricane and an earthquake?

But then, before my very eyes, a huge, robust minotaur appeared. I took a quick swig of my water bottle and sprinted off as if my life depended on it, as if there would be no tomorrow... I wondered if there would be a tomorrow.

Calissa Chapple (11)
Brighton Aldridge Community Academy, Brighton

The Centaur Theory

The rain started without any warning, it was just meant to kill. With all that pollution we had made, it was our fault. The rain could melt you, like centaur blood. After the rain, people had become deathly hunters. To survive in this mess, survivors needed four things: water, food, shelter and a gun. I had everything I needed: a water distiller, food, a shelter and an assault rifle. The rifle was just an assurance against people that might try to kill me. People would kill to have what I had. But, after I saw what I saw, things changed...

Cosmo Calesini (13)
Brighton Aldridge Community Academy, Brighton

The Flood In The Room

It all happened all of a sudden. Water started to leak from the pipe inside the room. We quickly went to open the living room door, but it was jammed, so were the windows. The water started to get higher and we couldn't call for help. All our devices were malfunctioning. In a corner, my little brother started screaming, my mother was going to get cold water shock. I was panicking to such an extent that I couldn't think. I wildly threw my blue centaur badge towards the window, cracking it. Would the water leak out on time?

Maha Elnouri (11)
Brighton Aldridge Community Academy, Brighton

The Big Meltdown

It was a day like any other, the same as it always was. Then, ash floated onto my apartment window. My mum screamed at me to get out of here, but I wouldn't. The air was filled with the smell of bonfires. I felt the ground shaking. People fell down. Suddenly, the volcano exploded and flashes of fiery red and orange spewed everywhere. I realised that I had my satellite phone and pressed the buttons.

A helicopter arrived in an hour. I was then flown away to a place I didn't know, but I was glad because I was safe...

Ellie Richards (13)
Brighton Aldridge Community Academy, Brighton

Monster Hero

It was the last day of school and Kay was going to town with her friends without knowing the weather forecast. An earthquake was going to happen. It shook, it rumbled and it scared people. She screamed, she cried and she fell to the ground. Then, all of a sudden, a giant, red minotaur stepped into the light and picked them all up, taking them all to safety. It took them back to her house and, despite her broken arm, Kay was thankful for the minotaur's help.

Weeks passed and she was still friends with the minotaur...

Paris Marie Reilly (13)
Brighton Aldridge Community Academy, Brighton

Minotaur Tornado

During a horrific storm that was tearing buildings apart in New York, cars and buildings flew in circles, just to be launched into poor, innocent people. Out of thin air, a ruby-red minotaur blocked a car that was about to flatten a kid. At that moment, the minotaur had hit it out of its way. The Daily News building tipped and was sucked up. The minotaur ran to rescue the people. He pinned the tower down and tried to stick it down. He ripped out one of his horns and stuck the building down. He was then sucked up...

Aiden Whitton (12)
Brighton Aldridge Community Academy, Brighton

The Invasion Of The Neighbourhood

One day, in the quiet neighbourhood in California (called Ebby Lane), Ellie and her slightly older brother, Eric, were playing on their Xbox One, trying to break the world record for the most kills on Fortnite. All of a sudden, there was a knock at the door. It was Marlon and his younger brother, Kaleb. Eric rushed to the door to greet his best friend but, when Eric got to the door, he saw a glow in the middle of the road. He ran over to find glowing suits of armour and looked up to see aliens coming down...

Tia-Faith Phillips (11)
Brighton Aldridge Community Academy, Brighton

Jack And Minotaur

It was a cold, windy night. Everything was fine until the wind started howling. It got louder as time went by. There were strong buildings collapsing and everyone was screaming in tears. If only a miracle could happen...
"God, we need you!"
There was silence. It was worth a shot... I had to move as quickly as I could before I was squashed. All of a sudden, I saw a bright light. I saw a creature. It was a minotaur! The creature started pulling buildings up, God had listened.

Kamen Coulter (13) & Juan Bajel (12)
Brighton Aldridge Community Academy, Brighton

Flood

In the amazing place of Italy, there was a flood that everyone thought they wouldn't survive. The people in Italy were really scared, but there was this huge, red thing that came from somewhere, it was a minotaur. The minotaur was huge, red and strong. It could help any person who needed help. Italy was flooding and nobody could help because they were all stuck in their houses, the water was very high and freezing. The minotaur had come to help save them and take them somewhere safe...

Poppy Marshall (12)
Brighton Aldridge Community Academy, Brighton

The Day The World Changed

A tornado hit America, but it wasn't a small one, it was the biggest tornado ever. Before it hit, we had to prepare. Everyone was in a panic, breaking into shops and stealing food and guns to kill people over supplies.

Day three: My son and I are boarding up the windows and door. One day left before it comes...

Day four: We are so dead. I don't want to die. It's now hitting us. Our house was destroyed and my son is on the ground. I think I have to leave my son...

Ari Darbinean (11)

Brighton Aldridge Community Academy, Brighton

The Minotaur And The Girl

One day, there was a minotaur sitting in a deep, dark cave when suddenly, a girl (the queen) walked in. His life turned upside down when she walked in, the minotaur thought she was food and tried to eat her.

When the king went to go and visit the queen, she was gone. He asked the minotaur where she was and he said he ate her. The king decided to lock him up in prison but, when the minotaur was in prison, he decided that he should no longer live and killed himself...

Rosie Williams (11)
Brighton Aldridge Community Academy, Brighton

Code Name: Desolation

I was four years old when *they* came. The year was 3019. We didn't know what *they* were capable of. When it happened, I panicked. Volcanos erupted, spewing enormous amounts of glowing lava. Earthquakes split countries in half. We didn't know then that *they*'d done it, but *they* had.

Twenty years later, a few survivors remained, the rest had been taken away to who knew where. *They* took them in ships but didn't come back. *They* used Earth or its resources, *they* patrolled to make sure there were no survivors around to hear them, *they* called it 'Code Name: Desolation'...

Becky Lucy Todd (12)
Chailey School, South Chailey

Tornado Catastrophe

"There is going to be a colossal tornado," the news said.

Donald Trumpet's brain turned to ice. Wrinkles appeared on Donald Trumpet's forehead. It was hopeless. Donald Trumpet peered out of the window and stared. His eyes widened. Sure enough, people were standing outside. Scanning the frightened faces, he found out that it wasn't a dream. Sprinting down the staircase, he grabbed a massive supply of medical kits and gummy bears. Getting lost in the crowd, he generously handed them out to traumatised citizens. Everyone knew that they were going to suffer in the tornado... That was when it happened...

Keito Miney (11)
Chailey School, South Chailey

Nuclear War

The world was in turmoil, recovering from a series of airstrikes launched by the USA. Civilisations were destroyed and whole countries were annihilated, becoming lifeless wastelands. The eastern part of the world retaliated and destroyed America's government and military. My father was a billionaire and took precautions by constructing an underground vault. This where my story began...

My dad was a weapons researcher and made a full suit of power armour, Mark Four. The bunker was equipped with a swimming pool, cinema, toilets and five bedrooms. My family and I were cleaning the bunker when the alarm sounded...

Oliver Taylor (13)
Chailey School, South Chailey

The Galactic Snowy Mountain

"Argh!" I said.

"Keep going! I can see an avalanche!" said Ron.

"Oh no!" I said as I looked back. "Argh!"

I was covered with snow. I dug ferociously, trying to get out. It was freezing. Finally, at the top, I looked at Ron.

"Oh no! The whole world is covered in snow because of that galactic, snowy mountain," I said.

"Well, at least that solves global warming," said Ron.

"Look at that bear, he can't get out of the snow!" I exclaimed.

All we had was the bear, we were going to freeze or starve to death...

Elena Taylor (11)
Chailey School, South Chailey

Lone Survivor

I can't do this anymore. I'm so lost, so alone. They're all dead, every single person - gone. The Earth died with them. It is now nothing but crumbled buildings and abandoned cities. No more laughter, no more smiles, just silence, complete silence. It drills into my mind and drives me crazy. I can't do this anymore. I can't forget the despair in my mother's eyes as the life slowly drained from her body. I can't forget the screaming children in the streets as they desperately clutched their parents. I'm already dead. I close my eyes and pull the trigger...

Katja Von Der Becke (12)
Chailey School, South Chailey

A New Beginning

One million metres below sea level, the Earth's inner core erupted, sending a colossal shockwave which travelled quickly. In almost an instant, nearly all mankind had been killed. But a flaming inferno was yet to come.

In just an hour, Earth was lifeless until, in the air, a glimmering light appeared and wind whirled debris everywhere. A violent shudder shook the world as it landed, an enormous crater indenting the globe like a pit of death. Smoky mist surrounded the glowing meteorite as it fragmented. Out came a foreign colony, a new era had just begun for our Planet Earth...

Theo Crawley (11)
Chailey School, South Chailey

The Cut

Fifty years ago, people only had to worry about the welfare of animals when devastation happened. Now, we have to worry about ourselves. It's been a long time since I've seen non-synthetic foliage, long since I've felt safe. In my age, I've seen a lot, but nothing like this.

Peeking through the shutters, I see the lack of oxygen has gotten to most. I know I'm next. Everyone's days are numbered, people are suffocating every day in the outside world and there's nobody to protect them. We're the poison of our race. Change should have come sooner...

Sophie Mills (13)
Chailey School, South Chailey

World Wide Meteor Strike

It all just happened at once: first, all communication went offline, the world was in complete, utter chaos. Meteors were heading to Earth, the same thing that made the dinosaurs go extinct.

After the catastrophe, me and my neighbour, Michael, survived. Every now and again, we went looking for food and water but, because of the radiation from meteors, we couldn't get far. Day after day, we were finding fewer and fewer resources for survival. Soon we would completely run out of ways to survive, we may turn to cannibalism. Even then, the radiation would kill us in the end...

Ben Aldridge (12)
Chailey School, South Chailey

The Rumours

Technology. Why the constant need for technology? My whole life, I have been against it. Against phones, against TVs, against everything! Now, what's happened? Technology has taken over, a disease has spread, leaving anyone who looks at a screen dead. I have witnessed this in person. People I knew have... nevermind. But, if you refuse to stare intently at a screen, one of the infected will kill you by hand. For a while now, I have been running, running from the thing that was always rumoured to take over; well, those people who started the rumours were right, unfortunately...

Arwen Mae Weston (12)
Chailey School, South Chailey

Lucky Charm

I was alone, no one had survived. I didn't know what to do. How was I supposed to survive alone in the forest? I didn't think my life could get any worse. I thought my lucky charm might help me but it couldn't be very lucky if I'd managed to cause a forest fire that killed my whole tribe... Lying in front of me was my best friend. I really didn't know how I was going to forgive myself. Well, it was too late to do anything now... Suddenly I saw something... No, *someone*, moving... Another survivor! I wasn't alone!

Imogen White (11)
Chailey School, South Chailey

The Unfortunate Life

The wind echoes as the sounds of screaming children spiral around your head, the psychopath emerges from the body parts of unlucky people. You're in your room by yourself, or are you...? Around you, screams of souls whirl all around. The psychopath appears in the shadow of the hallway. You peer around the corner, someone taps your shoulder from behind you. You turn, nobody's there. You turn back. As you scream, you run, nearly having knives through your chest. You fall back against the wall, a knife slices your stomach. Your organs pour out, leaving nothing but flesh...

Alicia Williams (12)
Chailey School, South Chailey

Tsunami

The Earth trembled beneath my feet. Terrified, I peered out of the window, willing for the sight of the sea to calm me. Alternatively, it petrified me. A humongous, foamy wave was coming towards my village.

"Mum! Dad!" I began.

Then, the wave of salty, dirty water crashed into the house, ripping down the roof. Water surrounded me, filling my mouth. The sharp salt was too much. I heard a roaring sound in my head as my eyelids slowly protruded downwards. The water was everywhere, trapping me. A single thought banged on in my brain: *am I going to die?*

Rosa Linney (11)
Chailey School, South Chailey

The End Of Life

What had been seven billion people on Earth was now fourteen. They all thought that it would be impossible to rebuild civilisation and that all fourteen of them would die out, the human race becoming extinct. Their only means of survival was finding food in damaged shops, damaged by the explosions that had destroyed most of the cities, towns and villages. Their food supply was low and they wouldn't survive for long. All other living things were dead, so they couldn't hunt for food. Storms were now ten times worse because of the radiation... They wouldn't survive...

Leon R G Hargreaves (13)
Chailey School, South Chailey

Quick, Run

It flooded the whole city. The lava was red, the colour of fresh blood dripping down your body. It was running fast down the hill, into the cracks of the old buildings. My family had been downstairs, sitting on the new sofa we'd bought to go in the lounge. I'd been upstairs, lying on my bed, exhausted from last night.

It was around 2pm when I'd heard my mum screaming my name, "Holly! Get down here now!" I'd leapt off the bed, racing down the stairs when my mum had shouted again, "Quick! Run!" However, I'd been too late...

Felicity Stewart (14)

Chailey School, South Chailey

An Erupting Disaster!

The unthinkable had happened. An earthquake had struck Uraguay! Uraguay was closed and all I had was water, fruit and my passport. I was on the border so, at any time, I could use my passport to cross into Argentina. The earthquake wouldn't cross to there. I wouldn't be able to take my resources though.

Suddenly, I heard a rumble behind me, then the ground I stood on cracked underneath me... I didn't fall, but I couldn't move!

Days passed and nothing happened. Then, one morning, a small tsunami was triggered. I nearly got caught. I had to flee...

Fin Albanese (11)
Chailey School, South Chailey

The Significant Snow Storm

The worst thing that could've happened had happened. The majority of the human race was now gone, completely gone. All because of this powerful snowstorm that had significantly changed everyone's lives forever. Most people were squashed by their houses that had been torn down by the strong gusts of wind. However, the few people that had survived were trapped in their houses and needed to get out. My family and I were the lucky ones, we were all shockingly still alive but trapped. Every exit was blocked, the heavy snow had pushed itself up against every door...

Chloe Matthews (13)
Chailey School, South Chailey

Death Of All Earth

All you could hear were people panicking, shouting orders. There was a meteor heading straight towards Earth at a great speed. Was this the end? A giant, glowing ball was pulled towards Earth like a baseball.

Five minutes till impact. How could we stop it? Was it possible? We would have to destroy the meteor to reduce the damage, but how?

Three minutes left till impact. Now it was a flaming, red-hot ball like a Christmas ornament. There wasn't enough time, we needed to get to the bunker.

Five, four, three, two, one... The meteor had hit...

Jack David Lilley (13)
Chailey School, South Chailey

The Fate Of Ben

"I can't believe I survived!"

Ben sat down on the rubble, not believing that, only half an hour ago, an earthquake had torn down buildings and ripped deep gashes in the Earth like a child in a sandpit. Ben inhaled, then rapidly exhaled. He had lost his whole family to this earthquake and he wasn't going to let it get him too. He would survive, thrive and help the other survivors rebuild, recover and find company in people who'd gone through exactly the same devastation as them. As Ben got up, he suddenly saw someone on the cracked cliffs...

Gilmour Loader (11)

Chailey School, South Chailey

Death Of Human Race

Two people left on Earth, if you could still call it that. It was like a dried raisin. What happened, you may ask? Well, the sun went out like a lightbulb, just like that. No one knew how it happened. Everyone died, everyone except Noah and Sophie, who hated each other. But, they needed to get along to rebuild the human race. They thought they were close to getting the human race started again, but then, time stopped. The lights flickered out and they were plunged into complete darkness again.

"We're going to die," they said.

They were right.

Mia Walker (12)
Chailey School, South Chailey

The Lucky Ring

The ground shook and I turned. Planes and helicopters plummetted into Big Ben. Scared, I ran, anywhere but here. Every bus was being squashed by planes. A man came running towards me, I turned and bolted faster than a cheetah after a gazelle. Suddenly, my pocket knife fell out of my jacket. I grabbed it and hurled it towards the man. I clenched my only hope of light, my lucky ring. It felt like something from the movies, but much faster. Everything happened in a split second. *Bang!* I flew into the air. My ring flew into the distance...
"No!"

Hattie Duff (11)
Chailey School, South Chailey

Alone

I couldn't imagine how much I'd miss my family but, try as I might, I would never get them back. My life was great until one day, time stopped. Everything went dark, everything went silent. *Bang!* The ground shook. I didn't know what had happened until I heard the screams of families. I looked behind me and saw the one thing I was scared of: the end of the world. There were volcanoes erupting. The Earth was shaking, forests were on fire. The mesmerising yet devastating sights killed me inside. I couldn't bear the torture anymore, so I ran...

Molly May Sturgess (11)
Chailey School, South Chailey

The Falling

It was a normal school day, we were in our science class, ready for another hour of our boring science lesson on physics. But, this wouldn't be a normal day...

Suddenly, there was a flash of white then a whoosh and the world fell beneath me, revealing a bright, white background. Then a burning feeling came over me, then nothing... *Wham!* It felt like a brick wall had hit me hard in the face. I could barely breathe and pain ached across my body. Before long, I started to fall. Screams rang in my ears, something had happened, something bad...

George Harris (11)
Chailey School, South Chailey

Crumbling World

The ground begins to shake, people begin screaming. The surface of the Earth erupts into a huge wave of chaos. Large chunks of tarmac hit me, they shatter my feelings. I walk in devastation as the Earth crumbles around me. I am the only survivor for miles. Buildings crash, people scream, the Earth opens its soul. People fall through the cracks. It swallows innocent bodies, lives are lost in an instant. The entire population is wiped out. I'm alone. The smell of dead people fills the air, it wraps around me. Aftershocks hit me in waves. I begin to cry...

Joseph Braine (13)
Chailey School, South Chailey

Plan 42

Fire spread, everyone got on a plane. There was a plane crash on an uninhabited island, only five people survived. There was a baby, mom, dad, pilot and a demon disguised as Justin Bieber. The pilot walked up to the mom, dad and baby and had a chat on how to survive and what to do next. 'Justin Bieber' looked around because his plan was going perfectly.

The next day, the baby was missing. There was a horrible vibe going around the island. There was argument after argument until the next day. Someone else disappeared, Plan 42 was nearly over...

Isaac Mack (12)
Chailey School, South Chailey

Catastrophe 608

I woke up to discover something unbearable. On the street, my duvet melted. I put my feet on the concrete street and got a sudden pain, but my feet remained. I toughened up and walked, the air was filled with a green mist and the street lamps sparked with red-hot glowing sparks. I heard distant police sirens and saw some distant hills. I thought they were normal at first, but then I realised they weren't grass green! The hill was nuclear! The night sky was an illuminated purple. The stars were glowing. Suddenly, I gasped, my heart was slowing down...

Jakob Webb (12)
Chailey School, South Chailey

Earthquake

The city shook and the buildings collapsed. The people painfully roared, the quake caused people to hurtle into walls and later be crushed by falling objects. I scurried for shelter under a dark cave, chunks of trees falling on my hand like heavy rain. I lay there, deafened by the screams of people as they come to their tragic demise. As darkness engulfed me, I lay there unconscious.
Suddenly, I woke up. My body was bruised and bleeding. I limped over to take a peek around me. Suddenly, I descended and thought, *how am I going to get help?*

Mia Keen (12)
Chailey School, South Chailey

The End Of Life

Everything stopped, time slowed down. The world was ending but, there were two survivors: Harry and Jasmine. As dwindling flames fell from the smoky sky, people ran in vain for their lives. Earth was a ruin. The sun had exploded and now there was nothing left of it, just ash and burning debris. Harry and Jasmine huddled together like sheep in a storm. They only had each other now and they felt lost. Taking shelter under a bridge, they sat down to rest, not knowing that their survival would end in catastrophe, bringing the whole human race to an end...

Olivia Rachel White (12)
Chailey School, South Chailey

The Purge

The Earth's cracking into pieces and everyone's following the purge. It's mayhem, thousands of families are going to a vault that is supposed to keep out all diseases and dangerous people, but there aren't many spaces left so you'll have to hide away because people are going mad. 100,000 innocent people were already reported missing. Now Big Ben is being struck down by a mob of angry people. This isn't good. Survivors that find this, go to Vault 250. If that's full, go to a military bunker near you. Good luck, survivor...

Luca Marco Darienszo (11)
Chailey School, South Chailey

The Explosion

I entered the room, they were waiting for me. They said to get to London. I obeyed. Thousands were dead, families were crying at the corpses of their loved ones, fires were ruining homes, Big Ben was half-destroyed, it was terrible. When I saw what had happened, I started to cry. The screens were cracked but, at that moment, others were rushed into our troop carriers.

They were shouting, "Nuke incoming!"

I ran as fast as I could, but I knew it was no use. It would kill me. I stopped, got out a notebook and waited for my death...

Luca Tabatadze (12)
Chailey School, South Chailey

Alien Atmosphere

What's happening? Is it a war? They're coming closer. They're going to land! Lots of people are running outside their houses. There are aliens dropping bombs on us. They're bombing everywhere, it's on the news. They are aliens! Everyone's going to be killed.

Suddenly, there's fire and UFOs everywhere! We need to send them back to Mars before they destroy the whole world.

All my neighbours are gone. The whole village is dead apart from me and my family. That's it... The aliens have taken over the world...

Ava Frean (11)
Chailey School, South Chailey

On The Edge!

Have you ever wondered what it's like to live life on the edge? Well, I have ever since the California wildfires started.

Hi, I'm Alfie. I was a resident of Paradise, a small village on the west side of the forest. My home was destroyed by the raging fires, I've lost my mum and my sister, Alice, went mysteriously missing. I've fled to New York and stayed with an old friend, but I can't shake off the feeling that my big sister, Alice, is still alive. So, one night, when I sat in front of the TV...

"Alice?"

Lily Cottingham (11)
Chailey School, South Chailey

Playing In The Dark

Darkness, it looms like a secret promise. The sound of crackling rips through the air like bullets and fires roar, covering the sand-coated ground, lightning destroying corpses. I see her always, calling, screaming, running towards me and then, silence. It's lodged down my throat, suffocating me so I can't breathe. Pain, it takes hold of my every breath, my every sob, my every move...
Day 123, I think: There's no way of knowing. The sun never shines and darkness never leaves. I'm Ash, I'm one of the five players left...

Ebony Hunt (14)
Chailey School, South Chailey

Disaster

Mount Vesuvius had been dormant for centuries after the disaster that occurred in Pompeii. A series of investigations had taken place as to why people were so unprepared and why they didn't react instantly. New safety features had been added and people started coming back. I was one of those people. We were supposed to be prepared, but nothing could have prepared us for this. It spread like wildfire, engulfing society like nothing else could. The lava ran like a river, thirsty for the blood of the innocent. Civilisation changed that day...

Lenny Page (13)
Chailey School, South Chailey

The Worldwide Earthquake

I hear a loud crack and another large crevice appears in the ground. According to the man on the news, this is a worldwide earthquake.

It's been three weeks now, all the TVs had fallen into massive holes, pretty much everything has been swallowed up by the ground. I think I'm the only person here who hasn't been gobbled up. Darkness creeps around me as I get deeper into the night. Suddenly, I feel myself slowly tipping sideways and darkness starts looming towards me. I desperately try to stay standing up, but I can't...

Bella Thwaites (11)
Chailey School, South Chailey

Lava Flow

I wish the world was as it used to be. Now, it's just fire, destruction and devastation. You have to fight for survival. Most are dead or dying, others are trying to get off the island. As I'm running, I look back to see it melting everything in its path as it slithers down the town's roads. People who weren't fast enough are burnt alive from the heat of the lava. The world around us collapses before our very eyes. The water's so close yet so far away. Just three meters away, I spot another lava flow coming towards me...

Hollye Brodie (12)
Chailey School, South Chailey

No Cure

It was just a normal day on my way to work. There was thunder and then there was lightning, what a strange day...

I got to work and got in the same time I always did but it was only me, a cleaner and my boss.

I said to my boss, "Where is everyone?"

He said, "They all called in sick because there's a bad bug going around. As both of us live further away, we didn't catch it, but it has already killed millions of people across America."

Oh no. I was a survivor of this deadly virus...

Frankie Francis (12)
Chailey School, South Chailey

Running

I was running, I didn't know where or how long it would take me, but I wasn't going to let it get me. I wasn't going to die today. Unaware of what was actually going on, I panicked and tripped. As I fell, so did my confidence. Eventually, I managed to pick myself up to start sprinting again. I couldn't see anything through the smoke; I was walking into nothingness. The heat from the flames skimmed my face, I thought I was going to melt instantly. I didn't know what was after me, but I wasn't going to die today...

Maisie Johnson (12)
Chailey School, South Chailey

Tornado Catastrophe

I finally finished my work at Chailey School; the end of the week was over.

When I got home, I put my meal in the microwave and set the timer for five minutes. Going over to my television, all the electricity flickered on and off, I didn't think anything of it. When I turned my television on, it went straight to the news.

"A tornado has been heading for the centre of New York. It has already injured seventy-four people on the outskirts. Quick, leave! It's coming."
I could feel my heart beating. I ran.

Lexi Rea (11)
Chailey School, South Chailey

Yellowstone Explodes

We were just leaving the airport when we heard that Yellowstone had exploded because of a bomb. The lava was already halfway across the Atlantic when we left for France. We landed as the pyroclastic flow stopped. There were only 5,000 people left so I went and raided the supermarket and found good food and water for the shelter. People were scavenging in the streets. For once, the homeless had an advantage because they had all the survival gear needed. I tried to help people but then the pyroclastic flow continued towards the city...

Matt Carter (11)

Chailey School, South Chailey

Into The Depths!

Suddenly, everything went black. All I could see was the glowing flare of random sparks of fire shooting upwards, destroying everything in its path. A sudden news flash appeared on the cracked screen of the television. I stared in shock. The polar ice caps were melting. The whole world was going to overflow! It was up to me to sort this out, I would be the heroine of this tragic story! I stepped outside and could see a dark wave slowly creeping above the horizon. Could it possibly be that I was one of the only ones left alive...?

Jocelyn Care (12)
Chailey School, South Chailey

Oof 2.0

Screams and sparks were flying everywhere; bright orange and red ash covered the singed grass, car alarms deafened me. I looked around and I was alone, not a living thing in sight. I started to run through the gaps in the road. I was running towards the school when I heard a cry, I wasn't sure who it was, so I carried on.

Suddenly, I heard it again, so I stopped and looked around. Something ran and hid behind an overturned car, which was lying on its roof, wheels spinning in the air. Was it really him behind the car...?

Izzy Hickman (13)
Chailey School, South Chailey

Fire!

I heard a roaring sound in the distance. I turned around, there it was. Sparks of fire were flying from the deathly volcano. Lava started sprinting towards me. I should've listened. I should've run away. It was too late now. It started getting hotter. I felt it coming closer. I started to hear the sizzling of the lava, the screams of the people around me and then, suddenly, I could feel the burning heat of flames. It felt like a never-ending burning feeling all over me. I knew it was the end for me and maybe the world...

Ava Reece (11)
Chailey School, South Chailey

And Then They Came...

The Cold War ended in 1991. The world had nothing to be afraid of, in the end, nothing happened.

We had something to fear, we had *everything* to fear because the end of the world didn't happen in the 1900s, it happened in 2023...

It wasn't a very 'end of the world day', it was, in fact, my birthday. You had to give it to the world though, they timed it very well. We had just blown out the candles and then everything was blown up. The bombs had come and no amount of blowing could put them out...

Alex Payne (12)
Chailey School, South Chailey

Devastation Has Struck!

It was like a scene out of a book: everything was so still and silent. *This isn't so bad after all*, I thought. I was wrong. I had been walking home after a tiring day at school when there was a sudden jolt that threw me off my feet. I looked for help, but buildings were collapsing and everything was chaos. I didn't know if I was running towards the danger or away from it but then, everything went black. It didn't matter anyway.
When I woke up, it was like nothing I'd ever seen. What had happened?

Tia Fordham (11)
Chailey School, South Chailey

The Dangerous Meteorite Panic

The end was near, slowly approaching as a meteorite approached the land of the living. As time was rapidly flying by in panic and realisation, the only survivors (not from the meteorite, but the city panic) were my sister and I. The atmosphere slowly fell as the night ended and the sun started to appear. The meteorite had started making some odd movements, moving sideways and dropping quickly. My sister and I had been trying to find a way out. After finding a way out, we spotted a bunch of cars approaching to rescue us!

Edward Whitaker-White (13)
Chailey School, South Chailey

Mission Madness

I was in the shops with my friend, Georgia, when my phone rang. It was Mum telling me that there was a massive fire spreading quickly. We had to grab all the food we could and get home immediately. We got home and we grabbed our pets and we ran to our bunker.

Twenty-four hours later and the fire had been put out. We came out from hiding, everything was burnt. All of us were okay and our friends and their pets were fine.

The next morning, we found out that ninety-seven people had died and no pets were killed.

Grace Gregory (12)
Chailey School, South Chailey

Exploding Mall

Bang! It started as a normal day. Abi and Milley were happily shopping when there was a load of people running. They didn't know what was happening and saw smoke. Suddenly... *Bang!* They knew what it was. They ran. Wherever they went, there were more. Suddenly, another one went off next to them and hit Abi. She hopped to a shop and got help, but all the other shops were bombed, so they had to stay where they were. The shopkeeper looked outside, she looked scared. She yelled, "Help!"

Abigail Massingale (11)
Chailey School, South Chailey

Praying

My skin was pink and peeling, my bones felt like they were melting. The flames grew as the population shrunk. Each day, more people were engulfed by the smoke. My mum used to plaster me with a thick layer of suncream, now she and the suncream were gone and useless. Black fumes filled my lungs like a black cloak smothering me to death. The sun's rays beamed angrily down on Earth, revenge for what crimes we'd committed. I curled up into a ball and prayed, not to God, but to my family. I wanted to be with them...

Hebe Rowling-Ashworth (14)
Chailey School, South Chailey

Killed By Sky

Flashing lights and the constant crash of molten rock almost had me hypnotised with fear. In the distance was Sky. A feeling of relief flooded through me, but that was the least important thing now. The future of the world depended on us. I slowly moved my feet so I was in the perfect sprinting position I'd learned in PE last Monday. "Three, two, one!" Sky screamed.

I flung myself out of my flimsy cardboard box. I glanced up and saw a huge molten rock hurtling towards me. I then knew my fate.

Willow Shoubridge (13)
Chailey School, South Chailey

I Had To Be Scared Of The Dark!

The lights flickered out, there was no power anywhere. I waited for it to come back on and when it didn't, we all hit the streets. I smashed the shop windows and in conjunction with many others, raided the high street. I then retreated into the woods, tears cascading down my cheeks as I left behind the ones I loved. I set up camp on a flat branch in a tall tree. It loomed over me as I thought about the horrific night ahead of me. *Good Lord, I had to be scared of the dark!* I thought furiously...

Chloe Gray (13)
Chailey School, South Chailey

The Plague Of London

It started with a measly illness but then, people started dying. A lot of people died in a small amount of time. I'd always wanted to roam freely in London, but with nobody about, it was too dull to have fun. The cracked walls left memories of old London, the London before all the deaths, the better London.

I knew I would die to the plague eventually and could feel my life coming to an end. We all died sooner or later and this was my time and London's. London fell because of one small, deadly plague...

Lucien Bourgeois-Templeman (11)
Chailey School, South Chailey

The Water Attack

I ran over to the docks on the other side of the city. The freak dropped the bomb into the water. Before I could chase him, he sprinted into the mist. Beads of sweat were racing down my back and palms. As I looked down at the water, it started to bubble from the docks and overflowed. I had to run. Before I knew it, the water was reaching tsunami sizes and collapsing houses and buildings. My family was racing to the helicopter, my best friend was dying. As I reached the helicopter, I turned back. It was too late...

Edi Xavier-Venn (12)
Chailey School, South Chailey

Help Me

Day after day, they come on and off, earthquakes destroying the town. It was like the Earth was opening up! However, one day, it was terrible, it was a nine on the Richter scale!
I was in the Shard, the tallest building in the UK. The ground shook, the windows smashed. I looked outside, terrified, buildings fell. I instinctively knew this was where it ended for me. The Shard leaned and then shook. I was in the corner of the room, shutting my eyes when... I heard a helicopter! I got up and ran for my life...

Will White (12)
Chailey School, South Chailey

The Infection

I was scared, terrified. There was nobody around. I was alone. I couldn't hear a thing. It was dead silent. I hadn't many supplies, I didn't know what to do. I needed to find supplies, I wasn't prepared. Every step I took was harder, the disease would soon take over me. Everyone got this horrible disease, it took over the brain, you went savage, lost control. They tried to kill the uninfected. I needed to find a better weapon... I could hear a group of them coming towards me. I started to run...

Seb Sommerville (12)
Chailey School, South Chailey

The Last One Standing

As darkness fell upon us, fear was all that was felt and hope was scarce. The time had come and the human race was coming to an end. Black figures lurked in the background, ready to take a life. They had no pulse and their voices were silent but the air went cold when the soul of a figure was present. Everyone hid in hope to live, but hope was low and many were found. Stories said some survived, but most didn't. Now the story was true, the cries of pain were the remnants of hope of those who'd died...

Willem Gregson (13)
Chailey School, South Chailey

The Human Extinction?

Robert woke up, he did his daily routine and he went to his high school. For the fourth consecutive time, he was going to get a late mark. But, when he walked into class, he found no students and no teachers. No one else but Robert was in the room. When he looked outside and secured the room, he realised that there was a giant fire outside. Not an ordinary fire, not a campfire, but a circle of fire! There weren't humans around the fire, not animals, but demons, all charging at Robert. Robert was doomed...

Cameron Laing (13)
Chailey School, South Chailey

Isolation

A deafening noise woke me as if the world had split in half. Screams echoed down the street. What was this? I looked out my bloodied window: the street was flooded with bodies. I sprinted to my parents' room, they were gone. I ran out to my backyard. I didn't have time to think of what I was doing. I ran and ran until I'd finally reached silence in the depth of the forest. I fell to my knees, eyes swimming in tears. I felt nothing, there was nothing but complete isolation until I saw a figure...

Rory Macleod (12)
Chailey School, South Chailey

Jimmy And The Bombs

A chain of bombs exploded all over the world, spreading panic across the world. Sirens wailed across the city as flames engulfed towerblocks. My room was pitch-black and silent. I tried to ignore the sound of screaming. Pushing down my fear, I blinked at the harsh, orange glow. I ran down the fire escape. There were policemen stood at the bottom, gesturing for me to run faster. Then, there was a flash, a bang, then darkness.
I woke up surrounded by dead bodies and rubble. I slowly got up, shaking...

Sam Chamberlain (13)
Chailey School, South Chailey

The Giant Hamster Destroys The World

Jiya the hamster was born with all the other hamsters but, when Jiya was born, he was bigger than the others. Then Jiya had his food and became double the size of an average human. Then he went on a rampage and the first place he went to was the UK. He destroyed all the buildings and most of the people but had a few survivors. The survivors had heard, if they didn't find the animal-shrinker, the world would end. So, they ran and eventually they found it, but they didn't know where he'd gone.

Jacob Sayers (12)
Chailey School, South Chailey

Savage Saviour

It had been five months and there was no sign of anyone. The Empire had collapsed and redemption was lost. It was two weeks until the next wave of destruction came. The robots had eliminated anything that moved so, Peter and I had to stay completely motionless. It was strange that no one knew how the robots were activated and if they would ever deactivate. Peter's arm had been lasered off by the robots and he now had a bionic one. No one knew about it but me, I had to be really discreet about it...

Alastair Orwin (13)
Chailey School, South Chailey

Tornado Attack

There it was, a tornado warning. I was scared of what could happen next. I was going to get stocked up on food and water. Then, it hit. I took my dog with me to the shop in case either of us got scared. I decided to see how close it was to my house by going through shortcuts. I heard people screaming in horror as they ran to the exit. Turning and checking what was behind me, I saw my little brother and he came to me screaming, "Mum and Dad were killed by the twister! It's the end!"

Poppy Mae Kinch (12)
Chailey School, South Chailey

The Explosion

It was 21st May, the year 2051. Me and my friend, Fin, were at the cinema. The sun was shining, but not for long. We saw fireballs flying towards us. We ran to Fin's house. We were freezing, but Fin showed me his power source. It was amazing. We were warm and I told him I had a duplicator somewhere in the house. Parts of the sun hit Earth. We decided to wait a few hours before duplicating the power source.

We managed to duplicate the power source millions of times. We had restored humanity.

Timon Gajos-Weston (11)
Chailey School, South Chailey

Death By Saviour

"Hello and welcome back to Channel 4 news with me, Alan Kemp. Today we focus on the ferocious flood coating the volcanic island of Hawaii. We focus in from our helicopter on an unfortunate family of five, stranded on their very own rooftop. A team of our rescuers have been there for days, trying to rescue these unlucky souls.
Now a rope is being lowered from our helicopter to the family to save them from the coming, raging lightning storm looming above us..."
Zap! Bang!

Kieran Payne (12)
Chailey School, South Chailey

The Girl Who Went Missing

I was getting my baby ready for the day out until a shake of the Earth sent a chilling feeling up my spine. I started to panic. I grabbed two bags, my baby and my dog. I should've listened, but I thought it was okay.

I ran to the games room, my heart thudding at the tapping of my shoes. It was like the world had turned upside down. I ran to the furthest corner and thought about my family, if they would be safe. I could smell the unearthly smell of ash and smoke. Then, there was darkness...

Amelia Feldwicke (11)
Chailey School, South Chailey

End!

We had no food, no water and barely any air. We all knew the Earth was going to blow up when mud started to fall into cracks, sizzling in its core. So, instead of dying, I went to a spaceship to fly it to safety. I wasn't the only person who wanted to live, loads of people were there...

Three, two, one... Blast off! It was going well until the spaceship crashed. That was how I got here. Now, there was one thing I wanted to say before I died and that was to live your life happily!

Lucy Scrase (12)
Chailey School, South Chailey

Space Race

It was a normal school day, except for one thing: NASA was launching a rocket to Mars. It was a crazy thought that a man would walk on Mars. The rocket later veered out of control and, on the small, mini camera, people across the world could see a small mass of land. It was England, but no one knew until they saw the supersonic boom and the red glow of the reactor core. Our skin sagged, our faces collapsed.

"Muh," said Tony.

I was thinking it was the end... I was right.

Jim Goodyer (12)
Chailey School, South Chailey

Falling Sun

Me and my friends were walking home from school, the sun beaming down on us. The sun was burning down hotter than it had ever been before. Me, Max and Fred stopped, we felt the ground shake and the sun seemed closer than it was ten seconds ago. All of a sudden, the sun was too hot to be under, so we ran. Cracks started appearing all over the road and houses started burning, so we dived into a house that was half-collapsed. I realised Max and Fred were gone. I was going to survive on my own...

Felix Holt (11)
Chailey School, South Chailey

Last Two

Hi, my name is John and this is my girlfriend, Carlie. She's fearless and also loves to kill the zombies that are invading the Earth. We are in an abandoned shack and, at the moment, we only have a shotgun and a machine gun. I am writing this so if we die and someone finds this, they'll not make the same mistakes. We are in New York, trying to find some gas for our car to get out of here. *What was that?*
I think there's a zombie and it's going to eat my brain...!

Aidan Bradley (12)
Chailey School, South Chailey

Earthquake

It was a normal day, well, it started that way. I was just watching television and cuddling my dog when the television started to shake, then the room shook. Not long after, the whole house was shaking. I went outside to let the dog out in the garden. The floor was all cracked, so were the walls. I had my stuff packed because I was going on holiday. I picked it up and ran. My dog was coming with me. It looked like it was going to be a long-term trip, not just a week. I also needed shelter...

Evie Head (12)
Chailey School, South Chailey

Silence

Inspired by 'A Quiet Place'

The static of the TV was deafening and we heard the breaking of our door on the first floor. We were in the basement, hiding from them. We had realised the static was luring them here. I smashed the TV with my pipe wrench. the creatures relied on noise to find their victims and it moved at the speed of light. One cry and you were dead. My family knew we had to keep quiet. My wife had just had a baby, but it made too much noise to stay quiet. We needed a lot more people to civilise Earth...

Harry Michael Junior Newton (12)
Chailey School, South Chailey

The Wildfire

As I get to the shops, the big, heavy doors close and the shutters go down. A news reporter comes onto the big screen. I feel panic alarms start going off, that's when the forest fire starts. I hear screams, I hear barks and I feel panic set in quickly. Out of the shop window, I see the trees starting to burn. The sirens of the fire engines get closer and closer... That's the day the wildfire started, I will never forget that day, the day the human race was erased from existence...

Brogan Peters (11)
Chailey School, South Chailey

Volcanic Eruption

I had just finished watching my favourite TV show when, at that moment, I heard an ear-piercing bang. I knew exactly what it was. I dreaded to think this would happen. The largest volcano in the world had just erupted! I grabbed my backpack, my phone, some clothes and my trusty craft knife; now was the time to run.

I saw the lava chasing me. It was getting very close. I ran as fast as I could into the forest. There was a long river that broke up the forest. I had to get across it...

Oscar Hart (11)

Chailey School, South Chailey

Collapsing City

I was out walking my dog when, all of a sudden, trees started to fall down, car alarms went off and screams started to fill the dusty air. It was like an apocalypse was happening. I rushed over to the centre of what looked like the end of Paris. A massive snap, then a screeching noise went through my head. A massive shadow took over my eyes.

"Move!" I shouted when I saw my friend; he was about to be crushed.

I was too late. I lost my best friend. This was the end...

Tom Laurence Laver (12)
Chailey School, South Chailey

Alone

One terrible day, there was a big bomb planted in the ground. I was the unfortunate person who witnessed the world's end. Even worse, I'd survived, the only person to be left alive. There was no one else, just me, alone.

The bomb had been placed there by a terrorist group. They had threatened to blow up the world. When the day came, I remembered that, before they blew up the bomb, they'd shouted something. Then, there I was, stuck, all alone with no one but myself...

Adam Langridge (11)
Chailey School, South Chailey

The Wall Of Fire

As me and my family hear the screams of helpless people and see the giant wall of fire closing in, my legs begin to become tired, my family leave me behind. The wall of fire rolls me in, the smoke going down my throat and into my lungs. The blood dripping out of my mouth, my eyes start to water as I see my sister lying on the floor, barely alive. I pick her up, determined to catch up to my parents. I know I'm not far. I break out into a run, but it's still following me...

Harry Boreham (11)
Chailey School, South Chailey

Volcano Eruption

"We are at the scene of the biggest volcanic eruption in history. Molten-hot lava is oozing out of the volcano. We can all hear the decisive screams of families in the city. Rescue services are on the scene right now, trying to save all the young children and families involved in the biggest natural disaster in history. Police think it will take about two years for the whole thing to be cleared up. The dry, hard lava will still be there for at least another century!"

Beau Kidd (12)
Chailey School, South Chailey

Never Go Shopping

Me and my friends were going shopping. We were in Costa when everything started shaking. We ran out, but not knowing where to go. I saw my mum and ran over, but the roof crushed her... Red blood came out like a river. We left the building. A car drove over to us and we got in. As he was driving us to the airport, there was another earthquake and we had to leave the car. We walked the rest of the way.
Finally, we got there! We would be safe after we boarded the plane...

Mia Johns (11)
Chailey School, South Chailey

The Flood

The city was in ruins. After weeks of drowning in water, not much stood. Thousands of homes had been lost or destroyed; it was a sorry sight. Everyone worked together to rebuild their homes and villages. But, one question remained: what had caused such a horrendous flood? The air was silent and all was still while water trickled down the sodden sidewalks. As a survivor, I felt extremely lucky to be alive, though I was also very worried that it could happen again...

Iona Hainge (12)
Chailey School, South Chailey

Flood

The rain crashed onto the roof of my house, nearly smashing through; the water around me was up to my feet.

Two hours later, the water was almost up to my head. I opened my door and swam to the nearest skyscraper in the hope that the water wouldn't reach the top. When I got there, the water was like rapids. I climbed the stairs to the top with about twenty other people.

The water had nearly reached the top of the skyscraper now. Would it ever end?

Harry Barnard (11)

Chailey School, South Chailey

I Panicked

This is the place where I was born, well, it was before the earthquake...

I had just gotten off the school bus and was walking home when the ground began to shake. I panicked, but then it stopped, so I carried on walking. Then it started again and it shook more, trees and buildings started falling, so I did all I could do: run! I got down to my street and the houses were gone. I fell to the floor and cried as the ground began to shake again...

Molly Brown (11)
Chailey School, South Chailey

The Bang

There it was, a meteor in front of my eyes. It was the end of me. I stood on the beach, there was a big bang. I could see a big wave coming towards me. I ran as fast as I could, but I wasn't fast enough. The waves crashed against the shore. People died before my eyes. It was the worst thing I had ever seen. People running for dear life, I thought I was safe. I found a deep hole in the ground that I could hide in. It was the end of my life...

Jasmine Blake (11)
Chailey School, South Chailey

Death Of A Zombie Boy

There was a boy who was called Jeff and he lived in a mansion. He was asleep, dreaming of a zombie apocalypse. He woke up and there was a zombie on his head. He screamed and ran away, but the zombie came and ate his face. He was eaten alive. His mum and dad went there, but no one knew that he'd died. No one was there to revive him when he died. When his mum and dad got there, they saw him dead and they screamed and never spoke about him...

Alex Heasman (13)
Chailey School, South Chailey

The Apocalypse

I was one of them, the last survivors. I was at a party and then the Earth was collapsing beneath our feet and then the first zombie came out. I didn't know why, but I shot the Nerf gun at it and it fell, dead. Then that was what we all did, more came. Then the last one came out, it was massive. Being the person I was, I ran at it, so my mates followed, shooting at it but one didn't. He got in a car and drove at it...

Jacob Arbuthnot (11)
Chailey School, South Chailey

The Flood...

I heard a deafening noise crushing the inside of my brain. I felt relief as I finally took a deep breath and I knew I was out, but then, something hit me. My senses and instincts told me that something was coming. Beads of sweat started dripping down my scarred forehead. It was coming and, before I knew it, it was right on top of me. I tried to gasp for air, but I knew my time was up...

Noah Mason (11)
Chailey School, South Chailey

Pompeii

I see the mighty mountain squirting orbs of fiery magma. The aroma of burning flesh surrounds me as I run. Terrified, people's screams of terror and agony whirl around me. Searing, powdery ash sticks to my skin, constantly scorching me. The bitter taste of the dense, polluted, arid air is almost unbearable. Water on my toga that protects me as I run starts to dehydrate.

A man running next to me screams, "We have angered the gods!" before being consumed by the blackest cloud of ash that trails, burning my ankles. I fall to my blistered knees, my tears evaporate...

Harvey Buckwell (13)
Owlswick School, Lewes

Firefighter

I'm calling from the depths of history to tell my saga. I'm Jack, a fearless firefighter. My greatest challenge was to save thousands of people from a terrifying eruption. Lava was spitting on their flesh as they ran for cover, but their cover blazed. Fast-flowing lava engulfed them, swallowing the people running uphill to caves in the hill for cover, but the lava ran up to meet them. I ran to the top of the hill, full gear and breathing apparatus. I let down my flame-proof ladders, citizens climbed to safety. One child remained, screaming. I lifted him to safety.

Jack Mead-Pearce (13)
Owlswick School, Lewes

Run Or Hide

It was a very peaceful, sunny day, all of a sudden it began to get windier. Trees started to crack as the wind grew strong and fast, moving among shifting trees. Piles of rubbish were flying around my head, while the wind was thunderous. I could see rats running wildly and houses being torn apart. While running away, I could smell life, I was ravenous. I could hear car alarms, burglar alarms beeping and people screaming for help. It felt just as if you had lost steadiness and fallen off your feet, with no power over what was happening...

Jamar McGlashan (14)
Owlswick School, Lewes

Peppermint Saviour

Enlarged wasps, from the excess oxygen, hover above me. They're ready, remorseless and rimmed with venom. Shaking my insect repellant, I glare at the queen wasp who lounges on the skyscraper above. Her nest swings lazily from the building and insects eat everything around it. They've killed everyone and now they're feasting on pride. These fiends dance above this ruined planet.

Oxygen caused this. It killed everyone I loved, oxygen that should've encased humans away from death. Now, death has come. Strangely, the death of insects comes from something unusual: peppermint.

Luckily, my insect repellant has lots of it...

Izehi Ebhohimen (14)

St Richard's Catholic College, Bexhill-On-Sea

Zombie Apocalypse

"It's the end! Run! Hide! There's a zombie apocalypse caused by an explosion in Tokyo's science lab. Now, savage beasts known as zombies are on the loose! They've raided ships, planes, cars, trains and even houses. If you happen to encounter one of these zombies, do not confront them. There is no cure for a zombie bite. They will eat your brains and turn you into zombies. If you've been bitten, you will turn into one of them; dead on the inside and the outside. You won't be in control of your own body. There's no safe place anymore!"

Joshua Porter (12)
St Richard's Catholic College, Bexhill-On-Sea

Last Day On Earth

The dust blew over the ground that had been constantly churned up by hours of fiery balls pounding the planet. The human race was nearly, nearly extinct.

"Wake up, come on, get up!" Alex shouted at James, almost smacking him.

"Huh? What? What's the matter?" replied James, startled.

"There are only twenty-five survivors left. An asteroid hit a base, we have to get moving!" yelled Alex.

Alex and James eventually got moving towards a massive recovery centre in Cornwall.

"What was that?" questioned Alex.

Both heads looked up just as a big, fiery ball broke through the atmosphere.

Zachary George Charman (13)

St Wilfrid's RC School, Southgate

The Day Of Judgement

All I could hear was screaming, cries and prayers. The Earth's surface ruptured before my eyes, taking the lives of countless people. Was this the end? The end of humanity? The end of all earthly suffering.

"Sis, I want to go home," my brother mewled.

"I know, Jasper, I do too but we've got to find Mum and Dad, okay?"

Jasper imperceptibly nodded.

"Let's go."

Cautiously, we lumbered through the havoc, carefully avoiding the wreckage. Jasper was only nine years old and he still had to experience this. Suddenly, the Earth beneath us plummeted...

"Bye, sis..."

Tanya Sunny (13)
St Wilfrid's RC School, Southgate

The End

I was having fun, but it didn't last, everything changed at the click of a finger. The swing stopped swinging, the children stopped playing. Suddenly, the park was empty. The air turned black around me. Smoke filled the air, screams filled my ears. What could I do?

Without thinking straight, I ran home, faster than ever. My heart was beating out of my chest. I couldn't go on. Forcing myself to carry on, I thought of never seeing my family again. It overwhelmed me. Was this the end of the human race? Was I too late?

Lucy Allen (13)
St Wilfrid's RC School, Southgate

The Strange Man

I woke up cold, alone, scared and not knowing where I was.

"Mum? Dad?" I said, hoping someone would respond to me, but still no answer.

A chill ran down my spine as a hand was placed on my mouth. My heart was beating out of my chest, so I hit the person and I ran. I didn't stop until I heard the steps behind me stop. I hid behind a wall. I cautiously peered around the corner, hoping to see no one, but what I saw next was much worse... A gun pointed right at my head!

Bang!

William Atkinson (12)
St Wilfrid's RC School, Southgate

Is This The End?

It was the year 2026 when the virus got out. It spread from human to human, mutating them into horrible creatures we'd never seen before. We knew the death of mankind was edging closer and we had little time until they found us. Sooner or later, they would infect us. There was only about 6% of the population left, we needed to regroup and fight back with everything we had. If we found out how the disease got out, we might be able to find a cure. But, we would never know, we just needed to fight back...

Aaron Wright (12)
St Wilfrid's RC School, Southgate

Worldwide Catastrophe

It all started on a normal day just like any other when, suddenly, an immensely big meteor hit the face of the Earth, wiping out everyone but a very lucky few. They were surprised and scared but decided to try and find others. A man called Dave was still alive and decided to embrace the wipeout, turning to nature and rebuilding the human race. As soon as he got into the forest, he realised that he had nothing to eat or drink. He walked around, trying to find shelter. He found a seed and planted it...

Mason Slight (13)
St Wilfrid's RC School, Southgate

The End

I had no idea what was going on around me. I could hardly breathe or see, there was too much smoke and fire around me. The bombs had just been dropped from the sky. I looked around the corner of the building I was near. I saw a family, they were holding each other, savouring their last moments together in this world. The crying felt like an alarm clock. I felt sad, knowing all my life's dreams were gone and that I was never going to see my family again. This was truly the end...

Adam Houas (12)
St Wilfrid's RC School, Southgate

The Butterfly

2.37am.

"The Butterfly calling in, over."

"What's it like, Commander?"

"Beautiful, I can see La Terre up here."

"Commander, you don't have to call it that."

"I know. She's just so... beautiful."

"Calling out, Commander, over."

"R.A.U."

4.04am.

"MS, are you there? MS, I need connection, now! Dammit! MS, if you can hear me - Mayday! We're going do-"

4.19am. Cascading down from space, the Butterfly crashed abruptly, slaughtering everyone within a 1,000 miles radius, killing them all in their sleep - all except one butterfly. Everyone was dead. The Butterfly had crashed.

Patsy Burley (11)

Steyning Grammar School, Storrington

Descent Into Darkness, My Final Moments

All is gone. All is dark. Everyone is dead. No sounds, just silence. Boiling blood slowly runs through my veins. My skin is bubbling and my heart is burning. The filthy air is cold and bitter. The disease has wiped out all of humanity and has left me alone. Afraid. Broken. I shut myself away from the outside world.

I'm done for. *Cough!* Dying now is easy, watching the ones I loved die was the hardest. I'm writhing in pain now, there's no hope. Vision is blurry, everything is getting darker, death is here.

A voice? I'm not alone? Hope?

Tristian Berwick (13)
The Eastbourne Academy, Eastbourne

The Warming World Of Death

The weather had worsened severely, only a few people survived but, they weren't ordinary people: they'd been born with powers and they'd protect the world. Two of them were guardians of the universe.

"Come on! We need to find the guardians, they should be here!" spoke Crystal to the others. Crystal was a blue cat. The others were dogs.

"We need to look for a white-haired girl or a white wolf."

"There, over there!" said one of the dogs.

The white wolf glowed and walked over. Their adventures had just begun... Would they save the world from world-ending destruction?

Isabelle Clark (11)

The Gatwick School, Crawley

The Moon Is Crashing Down

Everyone was screaming and panicking, nobody knew what to do.

"Harry, what are we going to do?" said Emily.

"I don't know, just stay calm!" Harry shouted over all the screaming.

Suddenly, everyone went silent. A loud voice crashing down from a booming screen scared all the people. They needed a plan, fast.

Out of nowhere, loads of men with guns came out and started shooting at the moon, which was heading for Earth.

"Get down!" shouted Harry.

After thirty minutes, the moon split into pieces. But, there was a very large piece still heading for Earth! *Boom!*

Leilani Campbell-Salmon (12)

The Gatwick School, Crawley

Overgrown

The lumpy texture of the overgrown twigs stagger my every step, clawing, pulling my body down. Glancing up at the once-bright blue skies that our happy children played beneath, a blanket of overgrown claws and crooked hands grasp the world, shading us from the rays that once kissed our blessed skin with its pure lips. Our sun-deprived skin itches and aches, however, when our pointed fingernails lightly graze our bodies, flaky chunks fall effortlessly to the ridged ground. Families huddle tightly and tears trickle down their sorry faces. I don't dare look into their watering eyes. I would never...

Madison Membry (12)
The Gatwick School, Crawley

The Host

It was cold and dark when I saw that light. Groans were approaching houses, deafening screams surrounded my ears. People were running and sprinting to escape the unknown that followed. The blood of innocents and sinners filled the streets, houses, walls and the town. Nobody knew what they were, they seemed to take the appearance of a loved one or a friend. *They*, no, *it* spoke no words, no expressions. Once caught, it would bury itself within the host and control every action that occurred. What were they? Where did they come from? There was something outside my window...

Katie Steere (14)
The Gatwick School, Crawley

Run

A loud rumble echoed across the land. I turned and stared at the volcano. Rocks were crumbling down. Onlooker's faces were filled with panic. Again, the fierce volcano rumbled. Thick, grey smoke escaped the mountain. The innocent, blue sky turned miserably grey. There was a sudden eruption of bright, red lava. People began to run. They knew they had to flee their homes. Red-hot lava ran down the volcano rapidly, flowing through the streets. The town was under attack. I began to run. Fear was overtaking me. Time was running out. I couldn't run any further. I eventually stopped...

Zuleika Janay Skuse (15)
The Gatwick School, Crawley

Darkness

It'd been 250 years since an asteroid darkened the world. They were the last people left. They'd found each other while looking for a place to live. The darkness was disappearing tomorrow.

The next day, they went to the side of the mansion, but they realised that they would burn in the sun.

"Michael, thank you for being there for me. You've made me smile every day. I love you."

They kissed, but they burnt to death. They'd lived a happy life in the darkness. They'd been happy, just them two, but the one thing they'd wanted was to live...

Evie Jackson (12)
The Gatwick School, Crawley

Bomb Horror

Skye Jones and Millie Jones were in an alley, drinking cans of Coke as they hadn't noticed what was happening. Bombs were being dropped and were exploding, people screamed and the city burnt and collapsed. People were dying, but they hadn't noticed. A bomb dropped near them and exploded, followed by a loud bang as the ground shook. They dropped everything and collapsed. They looked around and screamed. All they could do was evacuate. They ran as fast as they could. They fought their way through black, toxic smoke. They were out, but several bombs surrounded them...

Zanab Fatima (11)
The Gatwick School, Crawley

Polluted To Death!

A few weeks ago, Alisha was casually spending her money on exotic cars and expensive plane trips. Each day, air pollution got worse. All the fuel and gas from her cars and planes were having a dramatic effect in China. The ozone layer was weaker and weaker, it was also getting extremely hot.

Alisha was getting very worried, people had died and everyone who lived in the poorer parts of China were affected. They had turned into mindless zombies! Alisha realised her mistake.

"I should have listened!"

Alisha packed her bags and hopped in her private jet...

Aqsa Akbar (12)

The Gatwick School, Crawley

The Christmas Star

2037, the last ever Christmas tree shone in Trafalgar Square. Hundreds of people had come from miles around to witness this spectacle, little did they know, they were being lured to their own funeral. In the heart of the crowd, a small girl on her father's shoulders looked up at the star on the tree and noticed a second star. She told her dad and he saw the gigantic International Space Station Mark Z travelling towards them. What followed was the near total annihilation of Earth. 8.1 million people were reduced to 2,000. Earth would never be the same again...

Evan Mills (11)
The Gatwick School, Crawley

Revolution

Alan was watching his favourite TV programme. Suddenly, the TV turned off. Alan was confused, then red writing appeared on the screen, stating, 'Humanity is a thing of the past. Time for a new revolution.'

Then Alan heard a knock at the door. It continued many times, getting louder each time. Then, it stopped. *Crash!* Alan heard the door break down, then a plague of aliens rushed into his house. They all stopped, slowly turning their heads towards him. All of a sudden, millions of faces stared with their deep, red eyes, watching, waiting...

David Patrick (13)
The Gatwick School, Crawley

The End

"Mummy? Are we going to die?" asked Kris.

"No, of course not, Kristopher. By the time we get to Venus, Mars will have hit Earth and we will be okay, hopefully," said his mum.

"What will happen when Mars hits Earth?"

"It will explode."

Kris and his mum were heading to the rocket to go to Venus. Mars was hours from hitting Earth, so they were able to get onto the rocket with everyone else and leave in time.

"I'm scared," said Kris.

"It will be okay, Kris... I hope."

Leo Alexandre Scarborough Gomes (12)
The Gatwick School, Crawley

Devastation

What do I do? Giant craters have started appearing around my house and I'm getting really hot all the time. I think my house is falling on its side. Mother and Jane haven't come back from the shops. I think they were crushed by tectonic plates or melted by the tiny volcanoes showing up around the area where I live. How am I going to survive this catastrophe?

I'm pretty sure that only half the human race is left at this point in time.

Bang!

Was that what I thought it was? *Sizzle!*

Oh no!

Ethan William Wallace (12)

The Gatwick School, Crawley

The End

Bang! The explosion was so loud, you could hear it on Pluto. The vibrations were felt throughout the oceans, even the tallest of trees shook. It was almost beautiful in its destruction and terror. There wasn't time to report it or run, only admire death hitting like a wave. As humans watched their souls crumble in a hostile takeover of their bodies, the gods and skies watched, laughing for they deserved this. Nothing was left but the ash and memory of what had been destroyed. In one second, the blink of an eye, everything was over...

Stephanie Gonçalves Da silva (14)
The Gatwick School, Crawley

The War That Destroyed

I have twenty minutes, I've been hiding for twenty years. I ran from the war and I'm one of the few people who've survived. The others either have a deadly disease or they died and turned green. When I ran, I hid in a bunker but about two weeks ago, it was destroyed and so was everything else. I'm now on the run. I think I'm near London, but I don't know. It's all destroyed. Wait... I see someone, he has some food...
"Hello? Do you have some food I can have?"
I think he's eating a person!

Maddison Perry (12)
The Gatwick School, Crawley

The Eruption

Boom! Bang! The Hawaiian volcano erupted. My mouth made the shape of an 'o'. Unexpectedly, a red and black substance came towards me. I panicked so much that I fainted. When my eyes saw daylight again, the lava was closer to me, it was pointless to run. *Will I survive? I'm scared, I'm going to run faster than ever before!* I passed through the crowds in the stalls and towns. The TVs were all saying about how quickly it was coming towards us. I just gave up hope and stayed where I was, waiting for it to hit me...

Lucy Elliott (11)
The Gatwick School, Crawley

The Earthquake

I felt the Earth shake. There were abandoned buildings starting to fall, offices crashing like unstable planes. I didn't know what to do. At first, I just stood there, not knowing how to feel. I felt scared, nervous, wanting to know what would happen to my life. It all happened as fast as flashes of lightning. The people were ants, scurrying away from the murders. The dust coming up from the buildings was thick. I wasn't sure if I would make it. As I turned, I heard a scream. My eyes widened and I ran as quickly as I could...

Aamani Parekh (13)
The Gatwick School, Crawley

Evacuate

I heard screaming and opened the door to see flames flying through the air, the colours red, yellow and orange. The volcano spewed out lava all over the village. The smell of smoke overwhelmed me. Lava was getting closer and closer by the minute.

"Evacuate!" called one of my close neighbours. She was an old woman, but she could run faster than all of us. We left and ran to the city.

When we got back, there was nothing but dust and the statues of people who were running to safety, stopped in their tracks...

Saffron Leader (12)
The Gatwick School, Crawley

I Heard A Scream!

Through the city of New York, a mighty earthquake struck. Debbie was scared, heaps of bodies, blood blocking drainpipes, leaving streams down the road. She quickly walked down the road and tripped over something familiar, it was her football, but only half of it. She looked around for the other half, but couldn't find it. She realised that the earthquake had killed most people. It was then that she thought how lucky she was. She'd survived this. She tried to find some other survivors in the mess. Then she heard a scream...

Emerson Mansell-Boakes (12)

The Gatwick School, Crawley

The Shrink Ray

No way! There's no way my English teacher just vanished! It all started this morning. My brother, Jack, was in science class, he wanted to be an inventor. He had a cover teacher and they put circuits together. Jack had a plan to make a shrink ray. He'd carefully planned it out and started making it.

Once he was finished, he tested his invention out. His hand slipped and he aimed at the teacher. She shrank and turned into a pile of clothes! He went around zapping teachers. The next one was my English teacher!

Evelin Sumegi (12)
The Gatwick School, Crawley

Crash! Bang!

Charles was enveloped with fear as a meteor was making its way towards his miniature town. Suddenly, a tsunami of screams echoed through the canyon. As Charles peered through his window, he saw families running like headless chickens, warning everyone about the incident. Then, a loud crash hit the red sand and blinded everyone as it made a mini tornado. Then, a zoom whooshed by his ear. Then... *Bang!*

As Charles opened his eyes with a struggle, all he could see was blood scattered across his body and on the floor...

David Kallil Pierazzo Shockenn (11)

The Gatwick School, Crawley

Run Or Remember

The temperature was rising. Everyone in town stood in front of the huge creation, waiting for the day it would blow up. They were infallible, we knew that this day would come.

As usual, I was exhausted. Waking up from a dreadful night, thinking about 'that day', I went to get breakfast. As I was going down the steps, the news was on and was saying it was approaching. Fear, tension and anxiety filled the air. I stepped outside into the feeling of the scorching sun on my face. Another day...? No, it was happening now!

Mercedes Ofori (12)
The Gatwick School, Crawley

Nuclear War

One year ago, something terrible happened. It was an argument between the President of the USA and the President of North Korea. It was a time when people didn't agree, when Kim Jong-un threatened America, they launched a nuke tasked to destroy any lifeform.

But I was still alive. Me and my tribe lived in a radioactive submarine. It was powered by next-generation technology that helped me to live longer. It stopped the radiation from dissolving my skin and I hoped that, someday, we would finally get out of this mess.

James Ruby (11)
The Gatwick School, Crawley

The More You Run, The Closer You Get

As the blood-thirsty zombies got closer and closer, I drew my gun from its holster and the girl with me jumped with anxiousness.

"Crystal! You have a gun?" she exclaimed.

"I knew I'd need it at some point," I replied.

I shot the zombie square between the eyes and we ran. The zombies followed us, but they were extremely slow, so we ran as fast as we could, getting as far away from them as possible. Just as we turned a corner, we heard a car pull up and the sound of a gun being loaded...

Caitilyn Jade Walker-Speirs (11)
The Gatwick School, Crawley

Alien Invasion

Blood-sucking creatures were everywhere, hissing and grabbing innocent people and killing them. Who knew when I was next? How did these alien-like creatures get here in the first place? I was sure it had something to do with the secret agency, they had been doing suspicious things lately. Two days ago, there'd been articles about toxic chemicals in Chicago and they'd also 'accidentally' let those alien creatures loose on Planet Earth today! The aliens were coming closer and closer, I knew I was next...

Shanelle Terblanche (11)
The Gatwick School, Crawley

After Party

As my eyes forcefully opened, I felt the heavy force on my chest pinning me down. I felt a slap of hot air on my face, shortly followed by the missiles of sweat rolling down my face. I heard the cracking before the wheezing of my breath. I panicked and struggled and the weight became heavier, stronger, enveloping me. I paused before trying a final time. Then, I saw the after party of the blazing sun: angry fire and crumbled buildings. Confused and starstruck, I realised what had happened and I'd survived... for now...

Liam Butcher (12)
The Gatwick School, Crawley

Death At Its Best

I stood in my room on my phone, texting. Then, all of a sudden, the floor started to shake and I heard my mother scream. Then I felt myself fall. My mother's screams stopped. Then I saw darkness. I was scared, but I was still breathing, still okay. It had been a few days since I had heard my mother's scream. I hoped she was okay, not dead. It was then I remembered my dad, my brother, my sister. I'd been in here since Monday, my phone had died on Wednesday. It'd been longer than a day. I was dying...

Chloe-Anne Bailey (12)
The Gatwick School, Crawley

This Sucks

It was dark in space, my alarm woke me up, telling me that I could go home. I called NASA, but nobody answered. I looked out my window with my mouth gaping. There, in the solar system, lay the biggest black hole known to mankind. I was horrified, I was frozen in fear. I couldn't believe my friends and family were dying and I was all alone. I'd survived because of my space journey. I thought, *this is the end of humanity.* I had no food, no water. I, John Mark, had lived a good life. *This sucks.*

Mikolaj Kostrzewa (12)
The Gatwick School, Crawley

Plane Horror

A few months ago, Millie Jones was in her room with her friend, Katie Miller, packing to get ready to go to the airport and get on a plane to Turkey. She was living a wonderful life, but that all changed.

There was just one more hour until they got there, so Millie looked out the window and saw that half of the plane had gone! She screamed. The passengers had to evacuate. They all had to put on their life jackets. Luckily, the plane landed safely, but her best friend was gone. That was the worst day of her life!

Molly Gillian English (11)

The Gatwick School, Crawley

The End Of The World

The world is getting smaller so we have to get NASA to investigate what's happening and where the darkness has come from. NASA soon comes back, saying that the darkness is from Mars covering the Earth, so that light can't come through. Also, the Earth is getting crushed because of Mars. Over two days, everyone prepares for what's going to happen. Everyone dies, except for me and my friend.

The next day, the sun comes back and everyone is still dead, then my friend dies. I am the last person left...

Tatiana Almeida (12)
The Gatwick School, Crawley

The London Flood

There has been a flood in my city. I am trapped in a skyscraper in London with my dog and my mum. We have a few bottles of water, a phone, food and a flare gun. There is no way to get down. Helicopters are flying around and we get their attention using the flare gun. "Yes!"
Finally, we are in a helicopter on our way to a safe place called Og Bog, which is a community centre where people who've lost their homes go. There are lots of people there, sad, depressed and run-down. We're safe now...

Harry Field (12)
The Gatwick School, Crawley

Darkness

200 years ago, the Earth stopped moving. Now Earth is still standing, but there's an announcement that says the Earth will start orbiting again after 200 years.

A few hours later, we start to see light, we start to get light-headed and feel sick. We see The Smiths (our neighbours) go outside, but smoke starts to come off them. They don't seem to notice. The eldest son starts to fall down, starting to turn to ash. Then, the whole family starts to run to our house, they die on their way to our door...

Thomas Edmonds (12)
The Gatwick School, Crawley

The Polluters

I remember the day they came vividly. They rose from the water and said they were sent by Mother Nature herself. Nobody could have foreseen these monsters converging from the sea. We tried to fight back; they were taking our lives like dropping flies. I was twelve when they came for us, they took us by surprise. We couldn't fight back.

These days, we hide out in forests. The rest of my family is gone. I only survive, I don't live. I don't have a reason to. I must fight, I must slay them all...

Dylan Bendall (13)
The Gatwick School, Crawley

Hurricane Diablo

Everything was silent, I didn't know what was happening. Suddenly, I found myself in a fiery fury of wind.

My friends said something like, "Jozef, wake up! Diablo has hit, if we don't run, we'll be burnt alive!" In the sky, there were red, scarlet-red clouds of wind, but what was the scariest was the unnatural shape in the middle. It was a skull making an unusual gesture like it was pointing at me. I ran, trying not to trip. I knew it was my mind playing tricks, I had to run...

Jozef Ghinn-Morris (12)
The Gatwick School, Crawley

The Tornado

The world was in a bad state the ground was flooded, the air was hot and a tornado was coming over. I ran on the damp ground with cars broken around me. The tornado ripped up roads and houses as tiles flew behind me. A car flew too. I ran quickly, my heartbeat rose. I stopped to catch my breath, it was very warm. I looked behind me and ran, it was on my tail. I was then lifted by the tornado.

"Where am I?"

I looked up and saw my little brother and sister blowing around near a house...

Ethan James John Jackson (12)
The Gatwick School, Crawley

Life Fading Away

It started when the asteroid hit, all light disappeared. In the year 1943, everyone heard that there was a chance of survival, the chance to be free again. Her name was Evie, she was willing to risk her life to be the discoverer of a new opening. She went out of the bunker, her heart thudding a thousand beats per second. A sudden burning sensation touched her, she felt weaker and slower. Her last seconds were full of gasping and spluttering. She faded away. The sun, so bright, had wiped her life away...

Charlotte Howard (13)
The Gatwick School, Crawley

The Salvatore Flood House

It flooded my home top to bottom and I'm stuck with Lara. She's calling my name but I can barely hear her. She grabs my arm and pulls me over to the door. She opens it, water floods the room. We swim out. I find it hard to breathe as the water presses against my chest, my lips turning blue. As I open my front door, I fall out, scraping my knee across the cement. I look up to see Lara laughing loudly at me. It's clear this is just my imagination. *Maybe it isn't*, I wonder quietly.

Loula Stammers (12)
The Gatwick School, Crawley

The Hunt

Centuries ago, there was the Great War. Survivors ran into the Earth, now we return to the surface. I am at the back as we near the top, my skin starting to burn. We see a man drop dead, his body smoking. We all stop, shocked by what we just saw. We see creatures and run. The hunt begins.

Some of us stay behind to hold them off. I turn, seeing them get ripped to shreds, then they come for the rest. The elders fall behind and get eaten. Younglings also fall behind, there's no chance for them...

Christopher Bourne (12)
The Gatwick School, Crawley

Adrift

While I was swimming alone, I looked back to the shore. I went too far. I decided to go a little further but, while I was swimming, I didn't see any mountains. It was dark, the sea was coming towards me. It came closer and closer every second. It was a tsunami. I could smell salt everywhere. I tried to swim away, but my breath went. It was chasing me and I was running away like it was a monster. You could hear dolphins screaming. My hands, legs and body were so cold because of the cold water...

Dilayda Er (12)
The Gatwick School, Crawley

Thin Air

Feeling out of breath, I swam to the shore. I couldn't understand it at first, but all I could see were dead fish. I managed to make my way through the blanket of dead meat. At first, I saw very little. It was mostly black. Then I realised, the sky had died! Everyone was lying as dead as a rock. I thought there was a plague, but I was wrong. I started feeling light-headed, I felt like I was going to faint, but I didn't. I could feel the oxygen fading from my body. I fell to my death...

Josh Wain (13)
The Gatwick School, Crawley

The Webbing

Earth was amazing until our water went. The once-blue world was now dust, danger and death. I was scavenging when I found a large container. I thought I'd found the jackpot. I was wrong. It was a pile of nuclear waste! I started running, other scavengers saw me running and ran too. I knew this was the end, running from the green tsunami. I couldn't outrun it. I closed my eyes and let it take me, but it didn't. I opened my eyes and I had webbing on my hands and feet... I was alive!

Luke Cook (12)
The Gatwick School, Crawley

The Asteroid Hit

As we were decorating the Christmas tree, we heard a noise. We looked outside the window and jumped because it was our cat, trying to get inside. We let her in and we finished the tree. We then got ready for a Christmas Eve party.

We heard a noise outside, I didn't care but my sister screamed. We looked outside the window, then we all saw an asteroid coming towards us. When it got closer, we started to scream more and more. When it hit us, there was silence. We tried to survive...

Chloe-Sue Jupp (12)
The Gatwick School, Crawley

No One Could Escape

I saw people screaming and saw lava on the floor. I closed the door quickly, it came under the door. The colour was orange, red and yellow. It got closer and closer. The smoke really did smell. No one could breathe at all. I didn't see anything through the smoke, which was white and black. I kept bumping into everything while I tried to escape. When I opened the door, the whole city was nearly full of lava. No one could see anything and everyone was being burnt. No one could escape...

Malak El Fakharany (11)
The Gatwick School, Crawley

The Morning Of Horror

One morning, I woke up panting for air. My head was covered in sweat. There was steam in the air. I looked left and right, I couldn't believe what was happening. It was like a roaring lion coming to hunt. The volcano that was meant to be dormant had come back to life! How was this possible?
I got up and started to pack things. I had no other thoughts other than thinking I was going to die. As soon as I opened the front door, I knew it was too late. What was I going to do...?

Lily-Rose Brock (12)
The Gatwick School, Crawley

Starve

The sky was grey and the world was silent. There was no sign of life, not even a sound to be heard. The buildings were unrecognisable due to how crumbled they were, everything looked the same as before. My stomach was rumbling as I had no food. Every single drop of water had dried up and my mouth felt like a desert. I decided to keep on looking for even the smallest sign of water, but I knew it was going to take a long time. As I was looking for water, I spotted something far away...

Brad Lewis Ryan (13)
The Gatwick School, Crawley

The Infestation

One day, on a cold, black day, I took a day off from work. It was cold and dark and I was strolling beside the River Thames. Suddenly, all the lamps in the street turned off and some shop lights turned off too, so I turned my flashlight on. Then I heard a buzzing. I looked up and saw lots of flies flying past me. I ran. I stopped running in an alleyway. There, I saw a homeless man with a radio. On the radio, it said that 10,000 rats were swarming England. It was an infestation...

Bernardo Castico (12)
The Gatwick School, Crawley

The Hurricane

One day, I was sitting on my bed in my bedroom, watching TV. But then, the news came on and it said there was a hurricane on the way and so I panicked. I called my friend, Aqusa, and asked her if she'd heard about the hurricane. She said yes. Suddenly, the TV switched off. Aqusa said her TV had switched off too. Then I went running downstairs to ask Mum and Dad, but they said they had no clue what I was talking about. Then I went outside and saw the clouds, they were grey...

Nabiha Anwar (11)
The Gatwick School, Crawley

Halloween House

We went to our new house. We were happy, but the house scared me. The house looked like it was for Halloween and I was a small child. I said to my parents to move again because it scared me. They said everything would be fine.

Things started moving in the night while my parents were sleeping. When I saw the objects moving, I ran to my parents' room and said to go into the living room because the stuff was moving. They came and there was nothing...

Ciprian Liviu Ilosvai (12)
The Gatwick School, Crawley

Dead Not Alive

This happened when I was seventeen years old, I was going to the gym three or four times a week. It was a Friday when it happened. I had missed my bus, so I started to walk. I was five minutes away when I heard a lot of footsteps behind me. I slowly turned around and saw a herd of people with holes in their clothes. Then, I realised they weren't dead, but they also weren't alive. I slowly increased my speed to get to the nearest house for help...

Christopher Miles (13)
The Gatwick School, Crawley

 Young**Writers**® — Est. 1991 —

YOUNG WRITERS INFORMATION

We hope you have enjoyed reading this book – and that you will continue to in the coming years.

If you're a young writer who enjoys reading and creative writing, or the parent of an enthusiastic poet or story writer, do visit our website **www.youngwriters.co.uk**. Here you will find free competitions, workshops and games, as well as recommended reads, a poetry glossary and our blog.

If you would like to order further copies of this book, or any of our other titles, then please give us a call or order via your online account.

Young Writers
Remus House
Coltsfoot Drive
Peterborough
PE2 9BF
(01733) 890066 / 898110
info@youngwriters.co.uk

Join in the conversation!

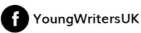 **YoungWritersUK**    **@YoungWritersCW**